Greenwillow
Read-alone

BARBARA ANN PORTE

Harry's Dog

pictures by YOSSI ABOLAFIA

Greenwillow Books, New York

Nesk

First Edition   10 9 8 7 6 5 4 3

Library of Congress Cataloging in Publication Data
Porte, Barbara Ann.
Harry's dog.
(A Greenwillow read-alone book)
Summary: Harry wants very much to keep Girl, his
new dog, even though his father is allergic to dogs.
[1.Dogs—Fiction. 2. Allergy—Fiction]
I. Abolafia, Yossi, ill.   II. Title.
III. Series: Greenwillow read-alone books.
PZ7.P7995Haq 1984   [E] 83-14129
ISBN 0-688-02555-2
ISBN 0-688-02556-0 (lib. bdg.)

to Venetia Colette Thomas
also, to my Aunt Rose and Uncle Leo
—B.A.P.

for Michal
—Y. A.

I, Harry,

am the owner of a dog.

Just since yesterday.

Last night I kept her

in the yard.

I did not have the heart

to tell my father.

I tell him now.

"Can I have a dog?" I tell him.
"Harry," says my father,
"don't you know I am allergic?"
Well, of course I know.
Anyone who's ever seen my father
in the same room as a dog
would have had to notice that.

First his eyes get red.

Then he sneezes.

It is hard for him

to catch his breath.

At least, I think,

he didn't say No.

"I guess I'll go outside," I say.

"Don't worry, Girl,"
I tell my dog,
outside in the yard.
(Girl is what I call her.)
"Everything will be okay.
I will keep you in my room.
Pop won't even notice."

I take Girl to my room.

We climb in through the window.

My father does not notice.

"Harry," asks my father

a little later in the day,

"did you hear something bark?"

He rubs his eyes.

"Not me," I say. "Did you?"

My father blows his nose.

"Harry," he asks,

"is something in your room?"

"My room?" I say.

"Like what?" I say.

My father opens my door.

"Like a dog," he says, then sneezes.

Girl looks at him and wags her tail.

10

client a little more power goes out of me. By teatime I am drained, my life-force is almost spent.' One pale hand drifted across her marble brow. 'And so, when I can no longer see into the mind of my sitter, or call up the spirits to interpret, I resort to other means.'

She fixed Clemence with a piercing blue gaze. 'A very little knowledge of psychology, a few questions, discreetly asked, and any one of us can learn all we need to know of another person. Do you understand me?'

'I – think so.'

'I am going to ask you if you, with your undeveloped powers, will help in this. For a consideration and your board, of course.'

Clemence was half-attracted, half-repelled. On the one hand it would be exciting to work in this realm of mystery, thrilling to find out people's secrets; and on the other the word Fishy rang insistently in her ears. 'But beggars can't be choosers,' she reminded herself. 'No more Missions for me, nor sweat-shops either, and it's that or slaving up and down with hot water and coal-buckets like that Annie.'

Aloud she said 'I'd like to try.'

Miss Pagenell beamed on her. 'How very wise of you, and how glad you will be one day that you trained under a medium of my quality. Sir Oliver Lodge, Sir William Crooks, Mr. Myers, Doctor Stainton Moses – I have sat with them all. The great age of mediumship is dawning, my child, with this new century, and you shall be its prophet.'

It was agreed that on Monday (no clients were seen on Sunday) Clemence should attend two sittings, to observe Miss Pagenell's mediumship under different conditions. On the Sunday night she hardly slept. People seemed to be all round her, voices speaking and laughing in her ears, visions in colours unearthly bright forming and dissolving behind her closed eyelids, snatches of music played. She woke feeling as if she had been on a long, long journey. At nine o'clock, half an hour before the first client was due, she presented herself in the Sanctum. Miss Pagenell, elegant in turquoise, was in position at the round table. She beckoned.

170

y father,

ep that dog.

e her back."

' asks my father.

"It is a long story," I explain.

"I have time," he tells me,

and sits down.

So I tell him my story,

the first one.

12

"I was outside," I say,

"minding my own business.

I was playing with my model plane.

Suddenly I heard a noise,

p-sssh, p-sssh, p-sssh.

It was a spaceship,

landing on the lawn.

Believe me, I was scared."

My father sighs,

or maybe wheezes.

It is sometimes hard to tell.

I go on with my story.

"Very short people,

with big heads and

little arms and legs,

climbed out," I say.

"In place of fingers, they had feelers.

A dog got out with them.

It was a normal-size dog."

"Harry," says my father,

"please."

"Yes," I say,

"that's exactly what I said.

'Please,' I said,
as loudly as I could,
'you cannot park your spaceship
on the lawn.
The grass will all turn brown.
My father will be angry.'

Well, when they heard that,
and saw how tall I was,
they got back into the spaceship,
p-sssh, p-sssh, p-sssh,
and left in a hurry.

Except for the dog,
who got left behind,
and followed me home,"
I say.

19

"Nice story, Harry," says my father.

His nose is running.

"Now tell me what really happened."

I tell him my second story.

"I was outside," I say,
"minding my own business.
I was going for a walk.
Suddenly I heard a noise,
v-room, v-room, v-room.

It was a car,
parked outside the bank,
with its motor running.

Six men sat inside, wearing masks
and holding baseball bats.
A dog was with them in the car.
Uh-oh, I thought, hold-up men.
Believe me, I was worried.

23

I called for help.
'Help,' I called.
'Police,' I shouted.
'Hold-up men.'
The police came
in their police car
with the siren on.

They arrived just as
the hold-up men
were getting out of the car.

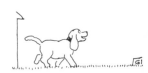

Well, when the hold-up men
heard the siren and saw the police
they all got back in the car,
v-room, v-room, v-room,
and left in a hurry.

Except for the dog,
who got left behind,
and followed me home,"
I say.

My father sneezes.

"Enough is enough," he tells me.

"Now tell me what really happened.

I don't want to hear

another story, Harry."

So I tell my father one more time.

"It is the truth, so help me."

"I am glad to hear that, Harry,"

says my father.

"I was outside," I say,

"minding my own business.

I was reading a book about dogs.

Suddenly I heard a noise,

beep, beep, beep.

It was Mr. Herman

in a moving van.

Mr. Herman *and* his dog."

"Really," says my father.

"Yes," I say.

"Mr. Herman leaned out

and asked me

if I'd like a dog.

Of course I said I'd *like* one.
'Good,' he said,
'because where I'm moving,
dogs are not allowed.'
Then, before I could explain
about your allergy,
he gave his dog to me,
and drove away in the van."

31

"I suppose," my father asks,
"he did not say
where he was moving?"
"No," I tell my father,
"he did not say."
My father puts his head
in his hands and reaches
for another tissue.
Just then the doorbell rings.

It is my father's sister Rose,
who lives two blocks away.

She owns a talking myna bird.
Its name is Molly.
"Molly wants a cracker,"
says the bird, every time I visit.
"Hi, Aunt Rose," I say.
"Hi, Harry," says Aunt Rose.

"You look awful,"
she tells my father.
"Do you have a cold?"
My father sighs.
"An allergy," he says.
"I have an allergy."
He points at my dog,
and starts to explain.
When he is finished,
Aunt Rose says,
"Poor Harry.
I know exactly
how you feel.

I used to think I'd die
if I couldn't have a dog.
Every time I asked,
your grandma answered,
'Rosie, don't you know
your brother is allergic?'"
Aunt Rose looks
as if she's thinking.

Then she says,

"Harry, I am not allergic.

If you'd like, your dog

could stay with me.

She still would be *your* dog.

You'd just take care of her

at my house."

I look at my father

to see if he agrees.

He puts his tissue
in his pocket.
"That would be wonderful,"
he says.
Then he looks at me.
I pat my dog.
I think I do not have
too many choices.
"Okay," I say.
"Her name is Girl,"
I tell Aunt Rose.
"She likes it when
you call her that."

I get Girl's leash
and give it to Aunt Rose.
"Here, Girl," she says,
and snaps it on her collar.
"Don't worry, Harry,"
she says to me.
"Everything will be okay.
I will keep Girl safe for you."
Aunt Rose kisses me goodbye.

Girl licks my hand.

"I will see you soon,"

I tell them both.

"You know,"
my father tells me
after they have gone,
"when I was your age,
I used to want a dog.
Every time I asked,
your grandma said,
'Don't be silly, Sol.
(My father's name is Sol.)
You know you are allergic.'"
Poor Pop, I think.
I am glad I have my dog.

41

"I think I'll go and walk my dog,"
I tell my father.

"That's a good idea," he says.

"Do you want to come with me?" I ask.

"Maybe just halfway," he answers.

When we have walked one block,
my father kisses me goodbye.
"Have fun, Harry," he tells me.
I wave goodbye, and hurry
one more block.

I am almost at Aunt Rose's.

I think about my father

and how he never had a dog.

44

I ring Aunt Rose's doorbell.

She opens the door.

"Hi, Harry," she says.

"Hi, Aunt Rose," I say.

"Hi, Girl. Hi, Molly."

Then I tell her my idea.

"Aunt Rose," I tell her,

"I want to buy a goldfish

for my father.

Will you help me pick one out?"

Aunt Rose smiles at me.

"Of course I will," she says.

"When?" I ask Aunt Rose.

"When would be a good time

to go pick out the goldfish?"

"Why not now?" she answers.

"Now would be a good time."

Girl wags her tail.

I get her leash and put it on.

The three of us are on our way.

BARBARA ANN PORTE is the Children's Services Specialist in the Nassau Library System in New York. Her stories and poems for adults have appeared in literary magazines in the United States and Canada. For children she has written *Harry's Visit*, the first Greenwillow Read-alone Book about Harry, and *Jesse's Ghost and Other Stories* for older readers.

YOSSI ABOLAFIA was born in Tiberias, Israel. As an animation director he has worked in Israel, Canada, and the United States. For Greenwillow he has illustrated *Harry's Visit* by Barbara Ann Porte, *Buffy and Albert* by Charlotte Pomerantz, and *It's Valentine's Day* and *What I Did Last Summer*, both by Jack Prelutsky.